Ladybird I'm Ready...
for Phonics!

Note to parents, carers and teachers

Ladybird I'm Ready for Phonics is a series of phonic reading books that have been carefully written to give gradual, structured practice of the synthetic phonics programme your child is learning at school.

Each book focuses on a set of phonemes (sounds) together with their graphemes (letters). The books also provide practice of common tricky words, such as **the** and **said**, that cannot be sounded out.

The series closely follows the order that your child is taught phonics in school, from initial letter sounds to key phonemes and beyond. It helps to build reading confidence through practice of these phonics building blocks, and reinforces school learning in a fun way.

Ideas for use

- Children learn best when reading is a fun experience. Read the book together and give your child plenty of praise and encouragement.

- Help your child identify and sound out the phonemes (sounds) in any words he is having difficulty reading. Then, blend these sounds together to read the word.

- Talk about the story words and tricky words at the end of each story to reinforce learning.

For more information and advice on synthetic phonics and school book banding, visit **www.ladybird.com/phonics**

Book Band 3

Level 9 builds on the sounds learnt in levels 1 to 8 and introduces new sounds and their letter representations:

igh ear air ure

Special features:

repetition of sounds in different words

short sentences with simple language

"Look, it's the fun fair," said Kim.

6

Mum said they might go that night.

"The lights from the fun fair are bright as we get near them," said Kim.

7

Story Words

Can you match these words to the pictures below?

fun fair	The Big Dipper
lights	secure

18

Tricky Words

These tricky words are in the story you have just read. They cannot be phonetically sounded out. Can you memorize them and read them super fast?

the	you	
said	so	have
they	was	I
go	to	we
me	are	like
come	some	what

17

summary page to reinforce learning

Written by Monica Hughes
Illustrated by Chris Jevons

Phonics and Book Banding Consultant: Kate Ruttle

A catalogue record for this book is available from the British Library

Published by Ladybird Books Ltd
80 Strand, London, WC2R 0RL
A Penguin Company

001

ISBN: 978-0-72327-545-9
Printed in China

Ladybird I'm Ready... for Phonics!

The Big Dipper

"Look, it's the fun fair," said Kim.

Mum said they might go
that night.

"The lights from the fun fair
are bright as we get near
them," said Kim.

"Come on The Big Dipper
with me," said Kim.

"It will go up high and you
might panic," said Dad.

The Big Dipper had pairs of chairs. Dad and Kim sat at the back.

Then, the man set the bar so it was secure.

The Big Dipper went up
like a rocket.

Then, it zoomed back down.

Kim's hair shot up in the air. Tears ran down Dad's cheeks.

The Big Dipper zoomed up
and down, up and down.

Soon, The Big Dipper
had come to a stop.

"What was it like up high?" said Mum. "Did you have some fun?"

"I did panic a bit," said Kim.
"But it was fun!"

Story Words

Can you match these words to the pictures below?

fun fair   The Big Dipper

lights   secure

Tricky Words

These tricky words are in the story you have just read. They cannot be phonetically sounded out. Can you memorize them and read them super fast?

the	you	
said	so	have
they	was	I
go	to	we
me	are	like
come	some	what

Ladybird I'm Ready... for Phonics!

The Silver Ring

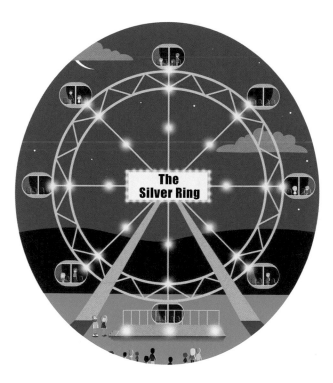

"Come and see the town from up high on The Silver Ring!" said a man with a beard.

All the pods have some chairs in them.

Mark, Dad and Mitch go up
the stairs and into a pod.

The man checks the door
is secure and off they go.

Up high, Mark sees the lights from the fun fair.

"Look, that is a church," said Dad.

"And I can see the park," said Mitch.

They are in a pod near the top. Bang!

Bang!

The
Silver Ring

The Silver Ring stops!

They wait and wait.

"We might be in this pod all night," said Mitch.

"We might be in it for years and years!" said Mark.

The man with the beard
checks the gears.
The gears need oil.

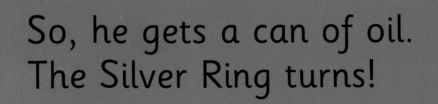

So, he gets a can of oil.
The Silver Ring turns!

Down come Mark, Dad
and Mitch.

The man tugs the door.
Mum cheers!

Story Words

Can you match these words to the pictures below?

The
Silver Ring

chairs

beard

church

fun fair

park

Tricky Words

These tricky words are in the story you have just read. They cannot be phonetically sounded out. Can you memorize them and read them super fast?

the	have	be
said	come	he
are	what	so
into	was	all
they	some	I
go	we	

Collect all
Ladybird I'm Ready...
for Phonics!

Captain Comet's Space Party

9780723275374

Nap Naps!

9780723275381

Top Dog

9780723275398

Huff! Puff! Run!

9780723275404

Fix It Vets

9780723275411

Dash is Fab!

9780723275428

Big, Big Fish

9780723275435

Dig, Farmer, Dig!

9780723275442

Fun Fair Fun

9780723275459

Wow, Wowzer!

9780723275466

Wizard Woody

9780723275473

Monster Stars

9780723275480

Say the Sounds

9780723271598

Flashcards

9780723272069

I'm Ready... for Phonics!

I'm Ready... to Spell!

Available on the App Store

Ladybird I'm Ready for... apps are now available for iPad, iPhone and iPod touch.

Apps also available on Android devices